Service Duty

Service Duty

BY DOMINIC N. ASHEN

4 Horsemen
Publications, Inc.

4 Horsemen Publications, Inc.
1497 Main St. Suite 169
Dunedin, FL 34698
4horsemenpublications.com
info@4horsemenpublications.com

Cover by Oxford
Typesetting by Autumn Skye
Editor Tilda M. Cooke

Library of Congress Control Number: 2023947119

Audio ISBN: 979-8-8232-0350-0
Ebook ISBN: 979-8-8232-0352-4
Print ISBN: 979-8-8232-0351-7

Table of Contents

Chapter 1

"**W**ait, you're really going to strap me into that thing?"

"That is the general idea, yes."

"Why?" I ask while staring at the contraption made of leather and wood.

"Ease of access?" Khazak offers as he walks toward the bench. I use the word "bench" loosely; it looks more like a sawhorse covered with padded leather.

"Uh-huh, and it has nothing to do with the fact that all the orcs in this city seem to be kinky bastards?" I've been on one of these before at our friend Brull's sex shop, but this one looks much more complicated. There are spots for limbs to rest and a *lot* more straps to hold them in place.

"That may have had a hand in things, yes," he answers with a hint of smugness.

"Do I really have to do this?" I whine but march toward my fate nonetheless.

"No." He looks at me like I'm stupid. "You also had the option of re-writing all the reports you ruined. You *chose* this. After being asked multiple times."

"…Only 'cause you didn't give me an option that wasn't spending the next two or three days writing," I grumble as I climb onto the bench.

"Mhmm, and I am sure it has nothing to do with the fact that you are *also* a 'kinky bastard.'" Khazak grins down as he begins to strap me in.

I know I'm complaining, but it's only because this time I really am innocent. At least partially—I'm gonna kill Nylan when I see him next. So, a while back, I played a prank on Khazak where I switched the ink on his desk with a pot that turns invisible a few minutes after drying. Ragnar and Nylan are the ones who put me up to it, and though I ended up with an angry Khazak and a sore ass for a few days, it was worth the laugh.

I hadn't really thought much about it again until a few days ago when Nylan asked if I'd do it again, this time to Ragnar. In return, I'd get to ask him for all the blowjobs I wanted for the next two weeks—our owners' permission notwithstanding. I figured I'd have to wait a bit to collect, but it sounded like a good deal to me, so I took it. I asked if he was doing this for a particular reason, but in his words, "Sometimes, a brat's just gotta brat." He assured me he'd take all the blame, though I agreed knowing I'd probably get in trouble for participating anyway.

I had a very simple plan for getting in and swapping the ink, which only required convincing Khazak to go in a little early one morning. It seemed so easy… until things went wrong. So, so wrong. What I didn't realize was that on *that* particular morning, renovations were beginning at the Tribal Hall—specifically on the wing that houses the office of Chief Grandtooth, the head of the city's militia *and* ranger force, and Khazak's direct superior. Because of that, the chief and his secretary, a man named Pragu, would be working out of our office until they were completed. Being the good employees they are, Khazak and Ragnar both offered their personal offices to their boss, and being the good boss he is, he insisted they only needed one—and chose Ragnar's.

Only I was not here for that conversation. After bothering Khazak to come in early so I could secretly switch the ink pots, I was sent on a run to the city's north gate to deliver a message about an arriving elven delegation. When I made it back, it was several hours before it even occurred to me to ask why Ragnar hadn't been in his office all morning. I started sweating when he told me the chief was using it, and then spent the rest of the day in a full-blown panic when I learned what he was doing.

I don't know the exact reason the delegation is visiting, only that it was related to some reports that the chief and Pragu were working with. As the reports are all written in Atasi, Pragu was translating them into Common to make it easier for the elves to read. Only he was using the disappearing ink I left on the desk. When the chief began to review his work and saw nothing but blank pages, he was first confused, then furious. Pragu obviously had no idea what occurred, but as soon as Khazak walked in and saw the ink, he knew.

To say they were upset is an understatement. Khazak thankfully took the brunt of the yelling for me, not that I could understand most of it anyway. Just the curses Nylan taught me, really. The chief is an intimidating man, standing a few inches taller *and* wider than Khazak with short gray hair and a grizzled face covered by a dark gray beard. He's got more than a few battle scars; his left tusk is broken, and there's a clean cut across his right eye from brow to cheek, the eye itself untouched. Pragu, though smaller, is no less intimidating, especially since he's still bigger than I am. His brown-and-silver hair is longer, pulled back into a tight bun, and he has a strong-looking, cleanly shaved jaw.

After things calmed down somewhat, I was offered a choice of punishments. My ass would be getting tanned by Khazak regardless, but to make up for what I had done, I could either rewrite all of the reports myself—with Pragu reading the translation out loud for me—or I could spend the day on "service duty" for the station's staff. I asked for clarification, and it's exactly what it sounds like—I'm going to spend the day tied down to this bench while rangers and officers take turns fucking me.

Part of me wishes I could say otherwise, but I didn't have to think hard about which option to pick. My hand cramps up just *thinking* about doing that much writing. So here I am, getting tied to a fuck bench with my ass facing the doorway. Khazak already told me the ground rules—no one will hurt me, I am allowed as many breaks as I need, and he will be constantly checking on me, so once he's done strapping me in, I think that's it.

"There." He pats my butt once he's finished with the final leg strap. "Any last questions before we get started?"

I rack my brain trying to think of anything I might have forgotten to ask about, my gut twisting when something pops into my head. "What happens if… What if a woman—"

"You will not be expected to service any of the women," he reassures me. "They will be more than happy to watch. Though I did hear a few of them asking Arik about his cock."

My body flushes, and I'm not sure if it's because I like or hate the idea. I shake it from my head.

"Alright, send in my first victim," I say with my head held high, or at least as high as this thing will allow.

"No need," he tells me with a laugh, walking around to my front. "He is already here."

"Aww, I thought we skipped morning sex today to save me the added soreness," I say with mock disappointment as I eye him unbuttoning his pants.

"No, I simply saw no reason to not sleep in a little when I knew this would be available to me all day." With a smirk, he pulls out his cock, already hardening and only inches from my face.

There are no more words as he closes the distance, and I wrap my lips around him. With my body strapped down like this, I can't do much in the way of movement, only able to bob my head slightly, so Khazak does most of the work. With a hand on the back of my head, he slowly pumps his cock in and out of my mouth. My cheeks hollow out as I suck lightly, feeling bold enough to tease it with my tongue once he is fully erect, swiping over the leaking, hooded head. Then Khazak pulls out, walking around to my backside with his cock standing out straight from his fly.

"We will need to make sure you remain well lubricated all day," he tells me as I hear the opening of a familiar bottle.

With a hand on one cheek to spread me apart, cool slippery fingers delve into my crack, making me jump when I feel them slide across my hole. They circle the area briefly before one presses inside, sliding easily down to the last knuckle, making me gasp. That first feeling of going from empty to full still catches me off guard no matter how many times I've been fucked. It does make it easier though, and Khazak soon adds a second and third finger, spreading them apart to ensure I am stretched to his liking.

"That should do it." The fingers are pulled from my body and replaced with something larger.

Both of Khazak's hands grip my ass as he pushes inside of me, one still wet with oil. They give me a good squeeze when he bottoms out, circling his hips around once before pulling back. He starts fucking me straight away, hands gripping me tight. I guess he *is* working, and not spending too much time fucking while on the clock is a very Khazak thing to worry about.

Seeing as I can't do anything but take it, not even move, I relax onto the bench. Khazak is well-acquainted enough with my hole by now that he knows *just* how to fuck me. Yeah, this is waaaaay preferable to spending the next three days hunched over a desk—because I'm sure it would take me a lot longer to write those reports out than it did Pragu. Sure, I might be a little tired and sore by the time we go home tonight, but I get to spend the entire day having sex! The choice wasn't even close.

"Oh good, he's already set up." I hear Ragnar's voice as he enters the room. "Do you mind if I take his mouth?"

"Not at all. That is why he is here today," Khazak answers, casual as can be while thrusting in and out of my butt.

"Thank you, Captain." Ragnar comes into view as he walks round to my front, hand already working to undo his pants.

As he pushes his cock into my mouth, he looks down on me with a hint of pity. Coming clean meant telling on Nylan, at least to Khazak and Ragnar, so he knows it's partially the half-human, half-elf's fault that I'm in this predicament. Not enough pity not to use me though, and soon he and Khazak are fucking me back and forth like a two man saw; when Khazak pulls back, Ragnar pushes in.

I feel like I'm being stretched to my limits. Getting filled at both ends is distracting enough as it is, but once Khazak start to work his fuck-magic, that becomes all I can focus on. His cock spreads my hole as it glides over my prostate again and again. I let out a muffled moan as I feel the little bursts of pleasure that accompany each pass. Then I feel a hand tapping against my cheek.

"Hey, pay attention." Ragnar emphasizes by thrusting into my mouth. "This isn't about *you*. Don't think I've forgotten that I was the intended target of your little prank."

I grumble unintelligibly around his dick. It's not like I can help it! Tell Khazak to stop being such a good top. Still, I go back to paying as much attention to him as I am Khazak. Not that anyone could really forget a *dick in his mouth*. I'm doing my best here!

Khazak's cock continues to feel amazing because I have no control over that. I do try to use it to my advantage though. Each time he pushes in to the hilt, there's just this smallest hint of pain, of being *too* filled. Whenever I feel that, I make sure to run my tongue around the hooded head of Ragnar's cock. *See? I'm paying attention!*

I'm surprised and a little disappointed when only a few minutes later I feel Khazak's cock pulsing as he cums with little more than a soft grunt. Our sessions normally last much longer, and usually by the time he's cum, I've had two or three orgasms myself. *Like Ragnar said, this isn't about you.* Khazak pulls out of me with a slap on the ass, pausing to admire his handiwork before leaving.

"He is all yours, Deputy," Khazak tells Ragnar as I hear him stepping away from us. "Try not to take too long. Chief Grandtooth is holding this morning's briefing."

"I will be there, sir!" Ragnar's hand leaves my head briefly, probably to salute.

Without another word, Ragnar pulls out of my mouth and circles around me to replace Khazak. I really don't mind. If I had to pick between the two, I'd choose getting fucked over sucking dick any day. Not that I don't like to suck dick; getting fucked just feels *sooooo* much better.

"If it helps, know that Nylan is being punished too," Ragnar tells me as I listen to him slick himself up. "Not quite as elaborately as this—he's getting spanked every night for the next two weeks."

"Thank you, sir. It does help a little." I never claimed to not be petty.

Ragnar follows in Khazak's footsteps and sets a quick pace right off the bat, the sounds of our skin slapping together quickly filling the room. Since I'm back to having only one orifice occupied, I can let myself enjoy it. I close my eyes and relax as Ragnar's thick length pounds in and out of my hole. He's not quite as big as Khazak, but he more than makes up for that in skill. I bite my lip to hold in a moan—I really don't want to make too much noise today. Whether that's to be courteous or just to hopefully prevent the entire building from knowing I'm back here, I'm not sure.

Khazak may have gotten me warmed up, but it's Ragnar who's going to push me over the edge. Each time he thrusts back inside, I feel pressure start to build up in my body, pressure that doesn't leave when he pulls back out. As things continue to build, I fight against the urge to tense up, knowing it won't be long before—*there* it is. Things crest and the pressure releases, and I cum with my face pressed against the padded leather to muffle my noise.

"Just can't help yourself, can you, boy?" Ragnar asks with a hint of cockiness.

"Afraid not, sir," I reply with a sigh, a dopey smile on my lips.

Ragnar finishes soon after that, tensing up as he breeds me and adds his load to Khazak's. He lingers inside of me a moment longer, enjoying the warmth around his softening cock before it slips out. After hearing the rustle of clothing, a cloth is wiped along my ass, Ragnar cleaning the excess lube and whatever else is dripping out of me. Then with a pat to the butt, I'm alone.

I'm not sure how long I'm in the "service" room by myself, but I almost drift off into a nap by the time Khazak comes back in to check on me. Walking around to my front, he holds a waterskin up to my mouth and allows me to drink. After putting it away, he moves to inspect my various limbs.

"How are you feeling?" he asks, checking the skin under the straps for irritation.

"Fine. Kinda bored. How long have I been in here already?" *It has to have been at least an hour or two.*

"About thirty minutes." *What?!* "I would not worry about getting bored. I wanted to check on you before the rest of the 'morning rush' came in, so to speak. You can expect more visitors soon."

With another pat to my butt, I am once again by myself. Before very long, I start to zone out, staring at a blank spot on the wall to my left. I don't even notice the footsteps behind me as someone approaches. It's not until I feel the hands on my ass and the deep chuckle that accompanies them that I realize I'm no longer alone.

"Well, what do we have here?" *That's Arik.*

Arik Deepfist is a ranger who, from what I'm told, lives up to his name. He also has a… well, magical cock. I don't mean he works magic with his cock—although he does that too—I mean it's a literal magic cock attached to a harness. While it doesn't cum in the traditional way, Arik still feels it like he is, but with none of the refractory period, and as a result, it gives him a stamina that is unmatched. Stamina that makes me nervous given how long I will be in here.

"You know the captain won't be happy if he finds out you spent the whole day in here fucking me, right?" I try not to sound too nervous, not wanting him to call my bluff.

"Oh, is that so?" Arik asks innocently. "Then I guess I better keep this short." I feel the heavy weight of his cock slap across my ass. *Did he walk in with it already pulled out?!*

There's only a brief moment where I hear lube being applied, and then Arik is aiming at my hole and shoving his way inside. It's suddenly a real struggle to hold in my groans, my hands balling up into fists. I kind of wish Khazak had left me with a gag, though I guess that wouldn't leave my mouth avail—*oh gods* that was at least another three inches.

"That's what I thought," Arik says with a slap to the rump after he finishes breaking me open on his length.

Content that I've been put back in my place, Arik fucks me in a familiar rhythm, his thighs smacking against mine steadily. My eyes are still shut, and I'm fighting to hold in my noises, but it *does* get easier to handle, eventually. But just when I start to relax, I feel the tapping of *another* cock against my lips and open my eyes to see … an officer whose name I don't know. Welp, I knew that was bound to happen today. The officer gives me an expectant look and taps himself against me again, inserting himself into my mouth when I finally open as requested.

The two begin to speak to each other in Atasi, and I am back to being used at both ends, though this time by very different men. Men who have a lot less patience for me than my owner and his best friend. It's not that they're rougher with me, exactly, but there's obviously less care in how they handle me—which really only serves to make the whole situation hotter. The way I can hear Arik laughing and joking like I'm not here, the way the man in my mouth doesn't care if he thrusts deep enough to make me gag. My body flushes red as I realize just how much the humiliation turns me on. That combined with Arik's never-ending pounding has me close to cumming again soon, and I cry out weakly around the officer in my mouth when I finally do, my hole pulsing around the solid weight of Arik's still-thrusting dick. And it just goes on and on. I'm not sure how many times I cum before Arik's finally had enough, but I can barely think straight.

"Alright, that is enough for now," he says with a sigh. "Not to worry. I'll be back after I finish some of that work you're so worried about."

With a few harsh spanks, he's gone, and the officer in my mouth moves quickly to replace him, another officer taking *his* place in my mouth. *Shit, does that mean there's a line?* Thankfully the cock currently in my ass is easier to handle, not even coming close in girth to any of the three I have taken already. It feels good, but I'm nowhere near close to cumming again. He cums himself not long after he starts, and I'm starting to realize I have *really* been spoiled when it comes to sexual partners.

I'm expecting the man in my mouth to take his place in my ass like everyone else, but he's content to stay where he is. I soon feel another person stepping up to my butt while my oral lover continues his steady face-fuck. His cumshot catches me off guard, filling my mouth with his load and forcing me to swallow or make a mess. He holds himself in place for me to finish cleaning off, then pulls out and leaves without so much as a thank you.

God, why did my dick just get harder?

And so my morning continues, with ranger after ranger using either my mouth or ass for their own pleasure. Some of them I know while others are total strangers. Before long, I'm not even bothering to look up at the orc attached to the dick I'm presented with. I just start sucking. Sometimes they switch from one to the other, sometimes they stick with a hole until they're done, but throughout it, I am at the center, offering up my body for their ill use. I'm still going to get Nylan back for getting me into this mess, but it would be a lie to say that I'm not enjoying myself.

I feel the officer in my ass pull out after cumming, and when he's not replaced and with my mouth free, I slowly come to realize that the "morning rush" has finally ended. I feel like a mess, covered in cum with both my mouth and my ass sore from all the use. The rest of my body feels stiff and is just itching for a chance to stretch. By the time I'm finally aware enough to call for some assistance, Khazak is already there, wiping me down with a warm, damp cloth and unbuckling me from the bench. After helping me to stand, he makes sure I drink some water before walking me to his office.

"How are you feeling?" Khazak asks after pulling us both onto the couch, one which has already had a towel placed over it. Good thing too because even cleaned up, my hole feels sloppy, and I know even if I tried my best I'd still leak onto the furniture.

"Good. A little sore. That was intense. But I, uh, also really liked it," I admit sheepishly.

"I hope you still feel that way after the second half of the day." He squeezes me into his side.

"Hey, David…" A quiet voice creeps through the open office door, and I turn to see Nylan sheepishly walking in.

"Hey." He looks afraid to come closer, but I'm too wiped to be angry even if I actually was.

"Are you feeling okay?" He steps closer, both of his arms behind his back.

"I'm fine, Ny. Really." I try to give him my best smile. Try. "But you definitely owe me for this. Way more than two weeks of blowjobs."

"*Blowjobs?*" Khazak repeats. "*That's* why you did this?"

"…Maybe?" Khazak only laughs and shakes his head at my answer.

"I brought you lunch!" Nylan finally shows me what he's been holding behind his back—two sandwiches wrapped in paper and a paper cone filled with *dar-buk*.

"This is a start," I tell the elf as I accept the peace offering.

Nylan nods, leaning in to give me a quick hug before scurrying out.

"Alright, enjoy your lunch. You get two hours today," Khazak says as I start to unwrap one of the sandwiches. "I suggest you nap after you eat to restore some of your energy. Chief Grandtooth made a comment about visiting you before the day was done, and I have a feeling you may need it."

I can't help myself and peer out of his office door into Ragnar's across the hall, seeing the man in question behind the desk reading. He looks up at me as if he could feel my eyes on him, a sly smile on his face. I swallow nervously, worried Khazak may be right.

Chapter 2

"It is time to get up, David." A hand on my shoulder gently shakes me awake. "Your break is over."

"Five more minutes," I grumble, trying to curl further into the couch.

"Well, I suppose we could always see about switching you to the overnight shift…"

"I'm up!" I roll over, eyes wide open at Khazak's threat.

"Good boy." He runs his hand through my hair before stepping back so I can sit up.

"How much longer do I have to go?" I ask, stretching my arms above my head.

"Three more hours." He offers me a hand to help me stand. "Come. I will get you strapped back in."

"Yessir," I answer with a sigh, following him out of the room.

As we pass through the station, I see people still coming back in from their lunches, and I feel more than one pair of eyes on me as Khazak leads me back to the "service" room. I know I saw more than a few of them before lunch, and they're probably all refueled now for round two. *This is going to be a busy three hours…*

Khazak pats the seat of the bench, which has been cleaned in my absence, and waits for me to climb on. I settle on my stomach, making sure my limbs are in all of the right places so Sir can begin the process of strapping them in. I appreciate them a lot more this time around—they might prevent me from being able to move, but they also stop me from worrying about holding myself in place. I can relax and focus on the tasks at … hole.

Speaking of… I shiver when I feel slick fingers running over my hole before pressing inside. I'm not exactly *sore*, per se, but I can definitely still feel all of the action from this morning. Thankfully, that means I'm a little easier to open up, groaning as Khazak applies more lube and scissors his fingers apart to ensure it is spread deep.

"I think you can expect a busy afternoon," he tells me after wiping his hand and bending down to my level (but not before I see the lump in his pants). "I will still be in to check on you, though you may not be able to notice me. But I promise I am here."

"Thank you, Sir." I nod as best I can. "I'll be okay. I can do this."

"Good boy." He smiles and strokes my hair again before standing and walking out. "Alright, men, he is all yours."

Seconds after I hear Khazak's final words, a pair of hands is already groping my ass. They squeeze my cheeks briefly before spreading me apart, and then the fingers are moving toward their target. Just as they start to brush around my hole, a third hand starts to grope me as well, at least until the first pair knocks it away.

"Hey, we can't *both* use his ass," the officer (Stonearm, maybe?) tells the interloper. "Go around and take his mouth."

The second officer does so with a grumble, already pulling his cock from his pants while making his way around to my head. He doesn't give me a chance to see who it is, just pulls my mouth to his cock, which by now has been trained to open automatically. As I help my oral occupant grow to its full length, the fingers in my hole press in for a brief moment, testing my tightness before they're gone and replaced with something much bigger.

I take a breath and exhale through my nose as the blunt head of my top's dick pushes inside of me. There's a quick pinch of pain as my body readjusts to being spread open, but then it's gone, and I am back to focusing on pleasing the man in front of me with my mouth. All the man at my rear needs is for me to stay relaxed and let him do his thing.

It doesn't take long before things start to feel good, and I'm letting out little moans around the cock in my gullet. It's grown to its full length, and its owner is using every inch of that length as he slowly drives it in and out of my mouth. A gentle face-fuck, if you will. My own cock is in the perpetual half-hard state it usually gets in when I'm being fucked. While the guy in my ass's pace remains steady, the one in my mouth gradually begins to pick up speed, until one of his hands is on the back of my head, holding me in place while he unloads directly into my throat, forcing me to swallow if I don't want to choke. I gasp for air when he pulls out, already tucking himself away.

"You take too damn long," the officer complains to his coworker as he exits the room. *What? No thank you?*

The orc (I'm assuming) in my ass doesn't reply, just laughs, and I don't get the chance to voice any complaints out loud when my mouth is once again filled by the last guy's replacement. Things settle back into place, with both men once again using me for their pleasure. A few minutes later, it's finally time for the orc fucking me to cum, pressing himself tightly against my ass as he breeds me with the first load of the afternoon. I whimper as he pulls out, air blowing over what feels like a gaping hole.

Another top smoothly transitions into place just as the one in my mouth did, and I settle into a rhythm, zoning out as I service these men for the remaining part of my punishment. I fall into a haze of submission and pleasure with my ass being filled, my prostate teased, and hands groping and squeezing along my body. All I can taste is cock and all I can smell is musk. I don't even bother keeping my eyes open.

The only time I get drawn out of things is when I get the first non-orc of the day stepping up to use my mouth—Ranger Hazatin, the dwarf, who has to use a small stool to reach the height of my mouth. As I swallow his dick down, which is poking out from a particularly hairy crotch, I realize he probably isn't the only one and has likely already been in my ass. In fact, I remember Nylan using something similar during my birthday party. I should really apologize for laughing at him for that.

Despite all of the non-stop action, I manage to stave off any orgasms of my own. It's not that things haven't felt good, but given how long the day has been and how much longer I still have to go, I just wanna try and keep my head as straight as I can. Gods know it only takes a few good ass-gasms to turn my brain into mush. I only realize the post-lunch rush is slowing down when my mouth stops getting visitors of its own. After the final officer has finished in my ass, I'm left lying there with the sweat, cum, and oil all cooling on my skin in the open air.

"Only two more hours to go," Khazak announces when he re-enters the room, walking around to my head to feed me some water. "Are you still feeling alright?"

"Yes, Sir," I answer after swallowing.

"Good because I think you can expect a pair of visitors shortly." He wipes my face with a handkerchief. "Chief Grandtooth and Pargu have just returned from a *very* long meeting with the Tribal Council, preparing for the arrival of the elven delegation."

Meaning my prank is probably fresh on their minds. "Thanks for the warning, Sir."

"You will be alright, puppy." He chuckles at my response. After making sure I finish the water, he runs a hand through my hair before leaving me. "I would clean you up, but it is my understanding that the chief actually enjoys a sloppy ass. I will see you in a little while."

And then I am left to wait, alone. I'm sure it's only been a few minutes since Khazak left, but it feels like forever. I get the feeling that the other rangers got the same memo from Khazak that I did, and none of them want to risk getting in the chief's way when he finally decides to pay me a visit. It's nerve wracking.

I'm spaced out, staring at a random spot on the wall while I think about what we might eat for dinner, when I hear two voices speaking as they enter the room behind me. Two older men, but since they're speaking

Atasi, I can't understand what they're saying. Still, I think it's safe to bet that my long-awaited visitors have finally arrived. While I mentally prepare myself, I hear one of them chuckle.

Two pairs of hands are suddenly on my body, groping and squeezing at whatever flesh they can find. They move over my ass, my thighs, my back, all while casually talking to each other. I shudder as fingers tease over the open entrance to my ass and jump when another pair strokes the soft skin of my thighs. The fact that neither of them has spoken a word to me has my already-hard cock pulsing in its pouch.

One set of hands leaves me, the footsteps of its owner drawing closer as he walks around to my front. A rough hand reaches out to grab my chin, lifting my gaze until I'm meeting the eyes of one Chief Grandtooth. He's an older orc, at least fifteen years Khazak's senior, and he has the grizzled looks to match. Despite his age, his body looks to be almost all muscle, his biceps bulging under the fabric of his shirt. His face is clean shaven, and his short black hair has already gone gray on the sides.

"After the trouble you caused, I trust you have been working hard to service the dedicated officers of this station today," he tells me with a stern expression. "And I hope my men have been working just as hard to ensure you have learned your lesson."

"Yes sir, I have. They have," I answer automatically. "We all … have." *What the hell does that mean?*

"I may require a report from some of them just to be sure." He strokes a thumb over my bottom lip. "I will also need to see for myself."

He releases my face, hands moving to the fly on his brown leather pants. I watch with anticipation as he unbuttons his fly before he reaches in and pulls out what might be the biggest cock I've ever seen. Like, I'm not sure my hand could fit all the way around it, and it's still *soft*. Are we sure this guy's Atasi name doesn't translate to Grand*cock*? Below it hang two large testicles, as green as the rest of him and covered in wiry black hair.

As I stare at this massive piece of meat in both wonder and fear, the hands behind me (that presumably belong to Pargu) finally dare to delve between my cheeks. I buck when two fingers slide into my slick and sloppy hole, meeting absolutely no resistance. He finds my prostate in no time, massaging it with the pads of his fingers while Chief Grandtooth brings his cock to my lips.

I have to open my mouth wide to take him in, immediately paranoid of scraping him with my teeth. He's still soft, but as he grows harder, that paranoia increases to the point of my jaw starting to cramp up. Grandtooth doesn't make a comment one way or another, just continues to silently slide his growing cock between my lips. He's so fucking big that I can't even try any of the tricks I've picked up with Khazak, solely focused on keeping my teeth away from his dick.

"Alright, time to see how your other end performs." He pulls out, apparently having had enough of the awkward blowjob.

I stretch and relax my jaw, happy for the break. Though of course, now my ass is going to be the one that has to contend with that thick slab. As the first pair of hands leave my ass, Grandtooth's replace it, his cock already prodding at my backside. Meanwhile, Pargu comes around to my head, lifting it to ensure that I look at him the same way I did Grandtooth.

He's got to be around the same age as the chief, his medium length brown hair also streaked with gray. He's wearing a pair of gold-rimmed glasses and looks to be about as tall as Grandtooth is as well. However, their builds are completely different, with Pargu being much leaner. His cock, which is thankfully smaller than the chief's, is already out, and my eyes flick between it and his face.

"So tell me, was the prank worth it?" Pargu asks with minor disdain in his voice, pushing into my mouth when I open to answer. "It was a rhetorical question."

I manage to hold off on rolling my eyes as I start sucking, not wanting to increase the man's ire. It *was* my fault that he had to rewrite almost everything he did yesterday. Mine and Ny's. Behind me, Grandtooth actively explores my ass with his fingers, slowly fucking me with at least two down to the last knuckle. When he pulls them out, I'm expecting them to be replaced with something *much* bigger, but instead, each of my cheeks is hit with a rough spank.

"Has Captain Ironstorm administered your corporal punishment yet?" After hearing his boss's question, Pargu pulls out so I can answer him.

"No, sir." After he speaks, the dick is immediately pushed back in.

"I may have to request that he do so here at the station." Grandtooth continues to tease and probe my rear, spanking me a few more times. "I think this ass will look much better after it has been turned a nice shade of red."

I feel both pleased and humiliated by the odd compliment, causing my body to flush and probably prove his point. Satisfied with his exploration, I feel him spread me apart with one hand while he uses the other to aim his thick slab of meat at my hole. My eyes scrunch up in pain as he tries to push inside because somehow, despite being fucked for almost the entire day, he still meets with some resistance. I can't help the muffled whine that escapes when he finally pops inside.

"Now you can see why I was willing to wait until the end of the day," the deep voice behind me rumbles.

I can, and I do, and I'm grateful for it. Chief Grandtooth continues to slowly push more of his cock into me, stopping every inch or so to give me time to adjust. Pargu is no longer fucking his cock into my mouth, content to hold it in my mouth, letting me breathe through my nose while I adjust. That or he's afraid I might accidentally bite it. After what feels like an eternity, the chief's hips are finally pressing against my ass, and I know I have finally taken all of him.

"Damn, that is nice." Grandtooth punctuates the compliment with a sharp *spank*. He then flexes his cock, making me squirm and cry out at the sudden increase in pressure in my hole, right over my prostate.

After a few more flexes, the orc in my ass begins to slowly pump his hips, barely pulling back a full inch before pushing back in. The orc in my mouth follows suit, though his thrusts are much shallower, possibly because he can still see the strain on my face. I'm not sure I've ever felt so full. Eventually, the cock in my ass begins pulling back more, and because of the over-stuffing he made sure to give me those first few minutes, the times when he bottoms out no longer feel quite so eye-bulgey.

Once both men sense that I am no longer struggling with what I'm being given, they return to their casual conversation from before, speaking in a language I can no longer understand while they fuck me back and forth. I have no idea if they're even talking about me, but when I can hear them laugh at their own jokes, my body can't help but burn red with embarrassment. The humiliation, the stimulation, all of it becomes too much, and before I even realize it, I'm cumming dry (ish, I'm leaking a *lot* of precum right now) on the chief's cock.

"Well, look at that." Grandtooth laughs as he fucks me through the aftershocks. "I had heard you were sensitive, but I am going to need to see that again."

He continues to fuck me, now with *purpose*, pulling at least ¾ of his cock out before sliding it smoothly back in. Whoever taught him how to fuck must have really known what they were doing because I am full-body shuddering on each in stroke. It's not long before I cum again, and again, both orcs chuckling above me in amusement.

I don't quite catch what they say—if they're saying anything to me at all—but at some point they both pull out, switching places. I can smell the cum coating Grandtooth's cock before he even presents it to me, pushing the loads of countless men into my mouth. He doesn't move much, still too large for me to suck comfortably for either of us, but I do my best. Behind me, Pargu slips into my open hole with ease, a happy sigh escaping his lips.

"You were right, sir. Even after everything it has been through today, his hole still feels wonderful around my cock," the older orc compliments me with a smack to my left cheek.

Pargu starts to fuck like he means it, like he wants to cum. He's fucking me with the full length of his cock, slamming it into me with every thrust. It pushes me forward a little each time, sliding me oh-so-slightly over Grandtooth, who for now is content to be slowly suckled on. Inches away from the base of his dick, the scent of cum soaked into his pubic hair, everything that leaked out around him as he fucked me, is all I can smell. I barely even notice when the thrusts behind me start to stutter, Pargu gripping my hips tightly as he thrusts into me a final time to add his load to count-less others.

"I do not know if that makes up for the additional work, but it was nice nonetheless." He pulls out of me with a gentle pat to my rear. "I am going to finish the last of the translations. Thank you for arranging this, sir."

"You more than earned it, Pargu." The chief pulls out as he says goodbye to his assistant, walking back around to my butt. "Now for the two of us to finish up."

He pushes back inside of me with a wet *squelch*, my hole once again feeling the burn of being stretched. I feel completely destroyed back there, and at the same time still stretched to my limit once he's seated all the way inside of me again. I whine unintelligibly, unsure of how much more of this I can take.

"Ssshhh." He strokes my sides gently as he shushes me. "Just a little longer. From what my captain has told me about you, you can take it. Make him proud."

I want to, *gods* do I want to, but the fuck that fol-lows those words might be too much. The pace he sets is fast and hard, even brutal. My hands clench and unclench uncontrollably, begging for something to hold onto. Hell, I'd even kill for a gag or a pillow to bite, anything to feel like I have something to keep me steady. I don't think it's even a full minute after he starts to fuck me that I cum on his cock again, and then again, and again. I seriously feel like my body is going to throw in the towel and just snap, when with an angry growl, Grandtooth slams home, breeding me more deeply than I think anyone ever has before, Khazak included.

My eyes are hazy and unfocused as I lay there. The only thing I can hear is both of our chests heaving as we catch our breath after that incredibly intense fuck. Once he is coherent, Chief Grandtooth grinds his hips against mine a final time, forcing a groan out of me before slowly pulling out. My hole feels so open and distended, and the cool air hits me with a rush, causing me to try and close my hole on reflex, and making me cry out at the soreness I feel as a result.

"Good job, boy." The chief compliments me with a final stroke to my flank. "As fun as I am sure today was, I think it would be best for you to try and avoid another one of these situations, yes?"

"Yes, sir," I manage to mumble.

With a laugh, he exits the room, leaving me alone on the bench, feeling like the definition of the word "wrecked." I'm just about to nod off when a hand on my back makes me aware of the fact that someone else is in here with me now. It's Khazak, who bends down to offer me more water as he wipes some of the sweat, spit, and whatever else has accumulated on my face. He waits for me to finish drinking the entire cup before speaking.

"How are you feeling?" He strokes a hand through my sweaty hair, searching my eyes for something.

"Am I dead?" Is that why he looks so worried?

"No," he says with a laugh. "But that looked very intense."

"Were you watching?" The thought makes me feel all warm inside.

"I may have been outside the door." He refills the water cup and offers it to me again. "I just wanted to make sure everything was alright."

"Thank you, Sir." I smile, taking another long drink. "Can you unbuckle me now?"

"Oh no, David. I am sorry, but you still have another hour to go." He grimaces as if there is *worse* news. "And I am afraid that while waiting for the chief and Pargu to finish, a large line has formed."

I groan loudly in frustration. *I'm going to kill Nylan.*

♥

"So what do ya think?" I watch Ragnar's face closely as he puts down my story, trying to gauge his thoughts.

"That was … very detailed." Ragnar puts down the book. "Between this story and the last one, it seems like you really like writing about David getting gangbanged."

"They say to write what you know," I respond cheekily. It *is* something I've been a part of before.

"Is that what that means?" he teases me. "You know the chief's dick isn't really that big, right?"

"Wait, you've seen it?" I grip him tightly on the wrist. "Why was I not informed of this?"

"Just when we were changing." He rolls his eyes at me. "It's not like it was hard."

"Well, maybe he's a *really* big grower." *Can't prove that he's not!*

Ragnar laughs and shakes his head, ignoring my comment. "I liked it. Even if you did kinda paint yourself as the villain."

"That's just to set up for the sequel," I tell him, wiggling my eyebrows.

"Oh, so you're planning a whole series of these now?" he asks, only half joking.

"I have *lots* of ideas for stories." I stick my tongue out at my owner.

"Whatever happened to the last one?" he asks about my story featuring David and Khazak's three fathers. "You never finished it."

"Oh." I scratch my head sheepishly. "Well, uh, after we had sex, I went back to read it and the idea of Khazak fucking David right in front of his parents was a lot less sexy when I wasn't all … hot and bothered."

"You realized you were going to have to look all five of them in the face again one day, didn't you?"

"…Maybe."

Chapter 3

"Where are they?"

"They'll be here soon. Calm down."

"They said they'd be here ten minutes ago!" I almost-snap at Ragnar.

"So they're running late." He shrugs and rolls his eyes. "What are you so nervous about? Wasn't this *your* idea?"

I've been pacing back and forth in our living room for the past fifteen minutes, trying not to stare at the clock. It's been a week since David spent the day on "service duty" for the rangers, a punishment he received as a result of a prank that I put him up to. He was just supposed to swap out Ragnar's usual pot of ink for one that turns invisible… but then it turned out Ragnar's boss, Chief Grandtooth, was borrowing his office that day. Needless to say, David ended up with a sore ass—in more ways than one—and to help make it up to him, I agreed to … tonight.

"Says the guy who isn't about—" A knock on the door cuts me off.

"That must be them." Ragnar gives me an amused look as he walks to the front door.

"Hello, Ragnar," Khazak greets his friend with a smile on the other side of the door.

"Khazak, David, come on in." He steps to the side and lets both men enter our home. "We've been expecting you."

"Can I get anyone anything to drink?" I ask as the two of them take a seat on one of our couches. "Water? Beer?"

"I'm good." David eyes me with a smirk as he practically prowls to his seat.

"I am alright as well." Khazak looks amused at David's obvious eagerness, setting his bag to his side.

"Khazak and I are going to visit a bar after this anyhow, so…" Ragnar pats the spot next to him.

"Great," I say, going high-pitched for a second. *Why am I so nervous?*

"So, you already know that as part of his punishment for his prank-attempt, I've agreed to let David 'borrow' Nylan for the evening," Ragnar starts to explain once I've taken my seat next to him. "But before things get started, I want to go over some ground rules."

"I'm all ears," David replies as Khazak sits next to him wearing a knowing smile.

"I'm giving you control of Ny, but I'm still the one in charge." My own sir points his thumb at himself.

"And I am still in charge of *you*." Khazak nudges his *avakesh* in the side.

"Which is why the two of us will be staying for the first hour and giving the orders," Ragnar continues.

"What? Don't trust me to know what I'm doing?" David challenges, his tone all teasing.

"My boy is a delicate flower, and I just need to make sure you treat him properly," Ragnar replies with a grin, pulling me into his side as I roll my eyes. "First, and this should go without saying, but you're not allowed to hurt him in a way that would seriously harm him or leave a permanent mark." He squeezes my shoulder, though I wasn't actually worried.

"What? I wouldn't do something like that." David is surprised at Ragnar's words.

"Good. Second, after we leave, no one else is allowed over here." Ragnar points to the front door. "I know you might be *sore* after having to take care of most of the rangers at the station, but that's not an option for revenge."

"Of course not. What exactly do you guys think I'm gonna do to him?" He looks between us and then to Khazak. "I don't even know that many people here."

"Look, it's just stuff I gotta say," Ragnar clarifies. "So that there's absolutely no confusion."

"Alright, understood, sir." David gives a silly little salute. "Anything else?"

"Just one." He reaches into his pocket to pull out a metal contraption he's only used on me a few times before—a chastity cage. "Would you like to do the honors?"

"Oh yeah, that's definitely going on." David nods with a wide smile, already off the couch.

"And staying on for a week!" Ragnar informs-slash-surprises me as he stands, handing the cage off to David. "He's all yours."

"Thank you, sir." David accepts the gift with a grin, then faces me. "Alright boy, strip and spread 'em."

"You're enjoying this *way* too much," I say with a shake of my head as I stand and do as I'm told.

"Like you aren't," he scoffs, crossing his arms and watching me strip with intent.

It doesn't take me long to get naked. We don't usually wear much around the house, just a shirt and some shorts, maybe some underwear. Which I may have skipped wearing tonight altogether since I knew this was happening. Just to avoid wasting time, of course. I toss what I am wearing to the side and return to my seat, spreading my legs wide as David kneels between them.

"Don't get used to this," he tells me as he slips the base ring of the cage down my shaft, which is already getting hard. "This'll be the only time I'm the one on my knees tonight."

"Is that a promise?" I taunt as he attaches the rest of the cage.

I shudder when my shaft is encased by the cool metal, making it lose some of its hardness. He quickly attaches the two pieces, clicking the lock closed before standing back to admire his handiwork. I frown at my groin and the attached cage.

"Alright, enough pouting," Ragnar tells me. "Why don't you two kiss and make up?"

David grins, wiggling his eyebrows at me once before pulling me into him and kissing me. He wastes no time, his tongue immediately seeking entrance into my mouth. I let out a squeak of surprise when I feel his hands move down to my ass and squeeze me roughly.

"Oh yeah, definitely spanking that later," he taunts me.

We make out like that in front of our men for a few minutes, David still taking the lead as he plays with my butt. I dare to reach one of my hands down and rub against his crotch, finding him already rock hard. The hands on my ass tighten as he grinds against my palm.

"I think you might be wearing a little too much clothing, David," Khazak comments as we break our kiss.

"I think you might be right, sir." David grins at me, already unbuttoning his shirt.

He sits down to pull off his boots, setting them to the side while he pulls off his shirt, pants, and jockstrap. He tosses them all onto a corner of the couch before retaking his seat, locking his hands behind his head. His hard cock points up against his stomach, precum already starting to gather at the tip. *It might be smaller than our orcs', but it's still a pretty nice dick.*

"Get on your knees, boy," Ragnar orders behind me. "Show him what you can do with that mouth."

Happy to do as I'm told, I sink to my knees between David's legs, spreading his knees with my hands. Since I wasn't given explicit instructions, I start by leaning forward and licking a stripe up the base of his cock. Then I wrap my lips around his head and swallow him down in one smooth stroke.

"Holy shit," David gasps, hand shooting to the back of my head.

I smile around the base of his cock, happy to have caused that reaction. I follow up by bobbing up and down on his shaft nice and slow a few times, my cheeks hollowed out from the suction. This is supposed to be part of an apology, so I'm trying to give him some of my very best work.

"He likes when you pull his hair," Ragnar sells me out from behind. "And he can hold his breath for a *surprisingly* long time."

I look up and lock eyes with David as he processes that information, his grip getting even tighter. He starts to guide my head as I move up and down his shaft, not quite trying to fuck my face, just letting me know he can. Each time I reach the base of his cock, he holds me down a little longer, testing Ragnar's boast about my breathing. *He wasn't lying.*

"Since we are talking about things people like," Khazak starts, "Nylan, pull off and move down to his balls. David: no touching your cock."

"Yessir," David replies without a hint of disappointment as I pull off.

I dutifully move my mouth farther south, nuzzling against the furry sack and taking a quick whiff of his musk. I start to slowly take my tongue over each of his balls, David's body shifting in response. He moans softly, his cock gives a nice twitch as I suck each one into my mouth. Out of the corner of my eyes, I can see his hands twitching at his sides, aching to touch himself.

"Good," Khazak praises me. "Now, move lower."

"Oh *fuck* yeah," David answers before I've even pulled his ball out of my mouth.

He lifts his legs, hooking both arms behind his knees as he bends himself in two to present his hole. He might be more flexible than I am. It's hard not to laugh at his eagerness, so I cover myself by doing exactly what I'm supposed to and eating his ass. Can't blame the guy for liking his ass played with. I am well acquainted with how good it feels myself.

I lap over the fuzzy hole, not missing the way he pushes against my tongue. I focus more closely on my target, running my tongue around the rim of his hole in slow circles before pushing all the way in. He moans, hands still around his legs, but I can tell he wants to grab his cock. His legs twitch every now and again as I tongue-fuck his hole, his toes curling.

"Alright, back to his cock" is Ragnar's next order. "David, let's see what you can do."

"You got it, sir," David replies, setting his legs down when I pull away.

He surprises me by standing up and pulling me toward his cock. At first my hands scrabble for purchase on his thighs, but I find my balance, trusting David to keep me from falling too far back. He thrusts his hip forward in time with the movements of my head, meeting me halfway each time he fills my throat.

"You know what I kept thinking the whole time I was tied up in the ranger station?" David asks me from above. "'I'm glad I'm the one doing this instead of Ny because there's no way he could handle it.'"

I look up and glare as best I can while getting my gullet stuffed.

"But I bet you would be fine if we kept it to just your mouth, huh?" he teases with a wink, holding my face against his crotch.

"You're probably right," Ragnar agrees. "He's been telling me about how badly he wants to blow Chief Grandtooth for *years*."

"Maybe we could set him up under a desk for a while," David suggests.

"You know, we've actually done that already," Ragnar reveals. "A few times."

"No shit?" David responds in disbelief.

"Have you ever noticed the way he sometimes seems to show up for lunch out of nowhere?" Khazak adds, revealing my secret.

"Fuck, that's hot," David mutters from above.

I (somewhat stupidly) didn't realize that Khazak knew that little secret, and I feel my body flush red. David very clearly loved the story, his cock seeming to grow even harder in my mouth. My cock tries to do the same in its cage but is of course just met with stubborn inflexible metal.

At the same time, the grip on my hair gets tighter, David fucking my face with almost the full length of his cock. I haven't gagged once, but drool is starting to leak out of my mouth and down my jaw. His balls slap against my chin in a steady rhythm, and I can barely see because my eyes are watering, but I can't lie—I'm loving this.

"You are really fucking good at this," David tells me, half-growling. "I'm getting close."

I moan as best I can around the cock in my throat, though I don't think that announcement was for me.

"What do you think? Should we let him cum?" Ragnar asks Khazak.

"Well, he has listened to all our instructions so far," Khazak reasons. "And I would like to get to the bar before it gets too late."

"Alright, you heard him. Feed my boy that load," Ragnar instructs.

"Yes, sir!" David happily agrees.

It already feels like he's thrusting as fast as he can, his movements getting more and more shallow until he's barely pulling even halfway out of my mouth. With his prick perpetually tickling the back of my throat, I have to focus harder on not gagging and timing my breath. It's a lot of work, but when I feel that cock start to twitch, expand, and then get shoved all the way into my throat so it can explode with a moan, I know it's all worth it. *God, I love sucking dick.*

David's chest heaves above me as he catches breath, his body still twitching as he rides out the last of his orgasm. Cock still hard, I suck out the last few drops of his cum, the rest of it already in my stomach. I know my face is a mess, but I still make sure to give David my best happy cocksucker smile when I pull off him with a soft *pop.*

"That was awesome." David sounds a little dazed, and he looks a little sweaty, too.

"I'll say," Ragnar agrees.

"Very good show, boys," Khazak congratulates us.

"Thank you, sir," David replies before helping me to stand. "You, uh, need a towel?" he asks, looking over my messy face.

"Yes," Ragnar answers, holding the one he was keeping at the ready just for this. "At least before I say goodbye."

He turns me toward him, wiping my face gently before leaning down to kiss me slowly. His tongue does not venture very far into my mouth, not eager to taste David's load, but I can still feel the heat behind it—especially when he reaches down to grab my ass. He likes seeing me used. When we break apart, I can see Khazak doing the same with David.

"David, I got you something special for later," Khazak tells him, reaching into his bag to pull out a smaller bag.

"Thank you, sir." David accepts the bag, looking surprised.

"Alright, you boys know the rules," Ragnar says as they start toward the front door. "We'll know if you break 'em."

"We will be back in the morning," Khazak tells us, throwing his bag over his shoulder. "Be good."

"Yes, sir."

"Yes, sir," we say in unison as they exit.

"Have fun!" David adds before closing the door. "I know I will."

"So… what's in the bag?" I ask, immediately curious.

"Lemme see." David opens the bag's flap and looks inside. At first he looks confused, but after reaching in and moving whatever it is around some, he's back to grinning widely. "This is amazing."

"What is it?" *Now I'm even more curious.*

"You'll find out," he tells me as he closes the bag, still grinning. "You know, I think I will take that beer now. Meet me in the bedroom."

Still naked with bag in hand, he walks down the hallway, all swagger. While part of me wants to smirk and roll my eyes at my friend's cockiness, the other part, the part locked in this damn cock cage, loves it. I sigh contentedly to myself. This is what I asked for.

Chapter 4

After filling a mug with beer from the kitchen, I walk it down the hallway to my and Ragnar's bedroom where I find David lounging in the center of the bed, looking smug. He sits up when he sees me come in, eagerly reaching for the mug and sitting back against the headboard as he sips from it. I stand by the side of the bed, trying not to roll my eyes.

"You know, if you spill any of that on the bed, Ragnar's gonna kill you," I tell him flatly.

"Well, I'll just have to make sure I don't spill then, huh?" he responds, taking another sip, cocky as can be. *Dammit, why do I think that's hot?*

"So, what can I do for you next, *sir*?" My eyes glance over his cock, which was shooting a load down my throat only minutes ago.

"Well, I'm gonna need a little longer before Little David wakes back up, buuuuuut…" He sets the mug

of beer down on the nightstand and flips over onto his stomach. "Get it? Butt."

I bite back a groan, glad he can't see me rolling my eyes. "Heh, yeah, I get it."

"Great." He spreads his legs and props his ass up. "Now why don't you get your tongue in there?"

"Yes, sir," I answer with a chuckle and crawl onto the bed. David has a very nice ass, and I am more than willing to spend some time rimming it.

I kneel over his upturned ass, rubbing my hands over his cheeks and the backs of his thighs. I'm pretty hairless, but David has this soft layer of fuzz all over his body that I love. Taking a hold of his butt, I spread him open, revealing more of the fur that goes all the way down his crack and over his hole. Grinning to myself, I move my face toward his ass and swipe my tongue over his hole.

David lets out a small moan of pleasure at the contact, relaxing into the bed. I lower myself to lay on my stomach, settling in as I continue to lick over his entrance. His ass still in my hands, I squeeze as I spread him even wider, pushing my tongue into his hole. He groans as the wet muscle breaches him, trying to move his legs farther apart automatically.

Still moaning, David pushes back against my tongue as I tongue-fuck him. I start slowly, pressing my tongue in as deeply as it will go inside of his furry hole and licking over it each time I pull back out. As I pick up the pace, I stop pulling all of the way back until eventually I am steadily pumping my tongue in and out of his wet and now relaxed ring of muscle. Pretty soon, David starts to shift on the bed, trying to get up on his knees and gain more leverage to ride against my face.

"Fuck," he says breathlessly, falling forward and turning onto his back. "Okay, I can't take any more of that. Time for you to fuck me."

"Uh, not that I don't want to, but…" I kneel and point at my caged cock. "Did you forget about the cage?"

"Nope!" he answers cheerily as he rolls off the bed. He bends over, reaching for the small bag Khazak gave him earlier, tossing it to me. "Put that on."

I open the leather bag's flap, peering inside to try and figure out what it is. *Is that a dildo?* I dump the contents onto the bed to take a closer look. It is indeed a dildo, a large one made of dark polished wood. It's also attached to something made of leather straps. What I'm looking at suddenly clicks in my head: a harness. It actually reminds me a little of the one our friend Arik uses—though I bet this one isn't magically enchanted to let the wearer feel the sensations.

I slide off the bed, David watching me as I bend over to step into the harness and pull it up over my legs. I adjust the straps around my thighs and waist so that it fits snuggly but not tight enough to cut off any circulation. I look down at the wooden cock resting on my groin just above my caged one and can't help but feel a little pathetic.

"Looks great," David comments after taking a sip of beer. "Now, lie on your back."

I get back on the bed as requested, my fake cock pointing straight up as I lay flat. David follows me back onto the bed, bottle of oil already in hand. He straddles my thighs and takes the wooden cock in his hand, inspecting its details before popping the cork on the oil.

"I think this might actually be modeled after Khazak's cock," he tells me while lubing the object up.

"The size is right," I add, noting the similarity myself.

"So does that mean Khazak had to stay hard and still for however long it took Brull or whoever to make this?" David asks, half-joking.

"They probably used magic, but yeah." I nod. "At least for a little bit."

After sharing a silent laugh, he finishes making sure my stand-in cock is sufficiently lubricated. David lifts up as he comes toward me, allowing it to pass between his legs. Now straddling my thighs, he reaches behind himself to hold the dick steady. He shifts backward, lifting his hips slightly as he finds the correct angle to push the toy in.

At least I assume because from my position I can't see much beyond his torso. So instead, I look up and watch his face: the way he bites his lip as he presses down enough to let it pop in, the gasp he makes when it finally does, the full body shudder he has as he sinks back onto it. My own cock throbs in vain inside of its cage.

David rocks his hips backward as he rides the toy, his half-hard cock splayed across my stomach. He moans low as he bounces on the fake-cock, the bottoms of his thighs slapping against the top of mine. Despite not being able to feel or see anything, I'm still driven by the urge to thrust upward and meet him partway. Sometimes, when he lifts up enough, I can just make out the toy disappearing between his cheeks.

Sensing my problem with not being able to see (or maybe just because I keep squinting at my crotch), David pulls all the way off with a smirk. Flipping around to face away from me, he restraddles my legs. Reaching behind himself to aim the wooden cock at his hole for the second time, he backs up toward my chest. I watch as the dark head of Khazak's copy presses against his already wet hole, forcing it wide when it finally presses in.

"Fuck," David comments as he takes more. "It might be the same size, but this thing's a lot stiffer than a regular dick."

As he sinks to the bottom, I notice the light sheen of sweat building on his back and reach out to wipe my hand over the warm skin. I feel his hands gripping my legs for leverage as he starts to ride me again, my hands moving to his hips automatically. From this angle, I can watch clearly as the dark cock is swallowed by his hole before being released, again and again. Locked away, my cock futilely fights against his metal prison, wishing he could take his rightful place.

I start to hump upward again, meeting his butt halfway as it bounces up and down. I can hear David starting to breathe harder, and I watch as his hole starts to pulse and flutter around the toy. His hands are tight on my thighs, just above my knees, squeezing me tight as he lets out a long moan as he has his first anal orgasm of the night. After pushing himself all the way down to ride it out, he lifts off and falls forward onto his hands and knees.

"Fuck me," he orders over his shoulder.

"Yes, sir!" I happily scramble up behind him on my knees.

I take aim at his now slightly-distended hole, gripping the tool attached to my harness tightly. David moans as he is stretched open again, arching his back eagerly as he takes it all the way to the base. I give his ass a squeeze with both hands before pulling my hips back, only to snap them forward just as quickly.

I fuck David with long, smooth strokes, pulling out about three quarters of the way before pushing back in. It doesn't take long before I start to notice the tell-tale signs of another impending orgasm, David's legs shaking when he crests over the edge. I keep up that pace for a solid fifteen minutes, giving David at least another ten dry orgasms, his chest falling to the mattress somewhere in the middle. As much as I wish I was using my real cock right now, I wouldn't be able to last even half as long.

Finally, after cumming for what is probably the dozenth time, he jerks forward with a full body shudder, pulling all the way off the dildo and flopping onto the bed on his stomach. His half-hard cock is splayed beneath him, pointed backward toward me, a thick string of precum leaking from the tip. I can see a damp puddle just ahead of me, underneath the spot where I had him bent over.

"Fuck, that was…" He seems to be at a loss for words, panting as he turns on his side to face me. "I'm gonna need a minute."

"Should I keep this on?" I ask with a little wiggle of my hips, the wet toy swaying back and forth.

"You can take it off. For now," he adds with a smirk.

After we both stretch our legs, we sit on the bed against the headboard. David sips on his remaining beer as we take a well-earned breather. This has already been quite the night, and it's not over yet.

"So, I gotta ask," he starts after putting the now-empty mug on the nightstand. "Why did you seem so nervous about tonight? I mean, I knew you were already being punished, but I still figured tonight was mostly supposed to be about fun."

"Well, I wasn't actually sure how angry you were," I admit. "I also didn't really know what you had planned for tonight. Even though I've been doing this stuff a lot longer than you, you're still able to take more of the rough stuff than I am." I try not to let any jealousy bleed into my voice.

"I mean I wasn't exactly happy about it, but it's not like you forced me to agree to pull the prank that got me in trouble," he tells me with a nudge to the shoulder. "Besides, if I'm being totally honest, the punishment really wasn't that bad. Kinda seems like something you'd normally have to work hard to set up. Willing to bet some people are actually jealous of me."

"You're not wrong." *I can think of a few friends who would kill for a rough ranger gangbang.*

"Alright then." He puts an arm around my shoulder with a grin. "Ready to have some more fun then?"

"Yeah." I nod, smiling confidently.

"Great!" he answers cheerfully, then pats his thigh. "Get over my lap."

I roll my eyes at the lack of a segue but move as requested, sliding across David's legs on my stomach. I'm spread just about across the full length of the bed, my head at the edge. David's hands roam from my back to my thighs, paying particular attention to his soon-to-be target. I get impatient waiting for the first smack to come and wiggle my butt to entice him.

"What, you *want* to get spanked now?" he asks before finally giving me the first one.

"Mmmf. Just wanting to get it over with, *sir*," I taunt, clearly not having learned my lesson yet.

He responds by giving me another two *smacks* in quick succession. After pausing to squeeze my ass to make sure I feel the sting, he continues to spank me on alternating cheeks. I'm not trying to keep count, but it's kind of the only thing I can focus on. Well, that and how much my dick would like to be out of this cage.

My ass starts to feel warm around ten, but things don't really start to hurt until around twenty. It's nothing unbearable, but it's enough that I have to start actively trying to not let out any noises of pain. Then around thirty I realize he might actually be *trying* to get me to make noise, and I stop holding back. He stops somewhere around forty, leaving me panting with a sore butt and a slightly more flaccid cock. David's, however, is hard against my thigh.

That really wasn't that painful, not even half as bad as the ones Ragnar has been giving me after I confessed. Still, when I feel David's hand on my sweaty back, I just breathe and relax. My ass is throbbing, and I'm in no rush to check the damage for myself yet.

"That'll teach you to get me in trouble," he jokes. "Now, turn a little and roll on your side for me."

With a stretch, I climb off of David's lap and turn diagonally on the bed. I'm still feeling a little warm and fuzzy, so I just plop down once I'm free of his legs. I can feel David shuffling around behind me, but it's not until he has me hike one leg up while straddling the other that I realize he's about to fuck me. The cock poking at my ass is a pretty good clue.

"Not too sore, are ya?" he challenges while slapping his hard dick against my ass.

"Not even close." I pull my leg up even farther.

"Good." I look back to see him spreading oil over his cock.

The wet head pokes between my ass just before David grabs me by the cheek to spread me farther. I whine at the contact with my sore skin but only try to arch my back when I feel him start to push in. I bite my lip as I'm stretched and filled, and when I feel his groin pressing against my ass, I drop my head to the bed with a happy sigh.

David gives me a couple of teasing smacks before I feel his weight shift, lifting his hips up to pull back before sliding back in. He's moving slowly, taking his time and really using every last bit of his dick. Ragnar fucked me this morning, and I'm still nicely opened up, so really it just feels nice.

When David starts to pick up speed, I can feel his balls slapping against my ass on every thrust while he rides me. Both his hands are on my butt, squeezing while also using me as leverage, his body weight pushing me into the mattress. From the angle I'm lying in, I really can't do anything else but take it and just focus on keeping my hole relaxed and open.

He's still using practically the full length of his dick, and every time it slides over my prostate, my own cock makes a futile attempt at growth in its cage. Soon, a familiar pleasurable pressure starts to build, and my hands fist into the sheets in preparation of what's to come. As the orgasm rolls through me, my body shakes, a bitten-off moan escaping my lips.

"Fucking *finally*," David says, exasperated. "I'm not gonna last much longer."

I keep my smart-ass comments to myself when David's rhythm suddenly changes to quick, shorts thrusts. A quick look back reveals his face is all business, and his balls slap against me steadily as he chases his own orgasm. The hands gripping my ass squeeze me even tighter when it finally hits, slamming his hips forward. His cock pulses inside of me as he unloads, the sticky warmth flooding my hole. After holding himself in place long enough to make sure he's expelled every drop, he dramatically collapses on top of me.

"Phew." He sighs into my ear. "Alright, give me like fifteen minutes, and we'll go for round four."

My ass is going to be really sore in the morning, isn't it?

♥

"So?" I ask Ragnar as he puts down my story journal.

"I liked it," Ragnar tells me honestly. "Kinda curious why you included all the stuff about being nervous, though."

"Every good story needs drama!" I defend. "Otherwise it would just be page after page of sex."

"That's a bad thing?" he half-jokes. "Isn't this like the third story you've written about fucking David?"

"Yeah, I guess. Why?" I look him over, curious at the line of questioning. "Are you *jealous?*"

"I'm not jealous." He rolls his eyes. "But it might be nice to read about you and your *actual* partner in one of these, once."

"At least you made an appearance in this one!" I point out. "The only reason I seem to have David on the brain is because of the last letter he sent me. It was filled with all sorts of details about all the kinky things he and Khazak have been doing on the road."

"Yes, and I'm sure reading about that has been very difficult for you." His tone is flat, but he's got a teasing look on his face. "Why don't we go to the bedroom so you can tell me all about it? Maye we can do some research for your *next* story?"

"Sounds like a good plan to me, sir." I grin. "Lead the way."

Property of:

Nylan

Book Club Questions

1. Have you ever gotten in trouble for something a friend asked you to do? What did they do to make it up to you?

2. Would you ever agree to something like David did, or would you have taken the other option: rewriting everything?

3. Before they leave, Ragnar gives David the ground rules on what he is allowed to do with Nylan. How would you feel in Nylan's place? Are there any rules you would want added or removed?

4. How would you have "punished" Nylan if you were in David's place?

About the Author

Dominic N. Ashen is an author and avid reader with a heavy focus on gay BDSM-themed erotica. After spending his youth in search of books with characters who were more like himself—queer ones, specifically—he decided to start creating some of his own. His writes feature queer protagonists, most often gay and bisexual men, and heavy themes of dominance, submission, and all sorts of kinks. Dominic loves the fantasy, sci-fi, and horror genres with a penchant for writing longer stories where he is able to weave in the sex and kink right alongside the plot.

Website: https://www.dominicashen.com/
Patreon: https://www.patreon.com/dominicashen
Twitter: https://twitter.com/DomNAshen
Facebook: https://www.facebook.com/dom.n.ashen
Instagram: https://www.instagram.com/dom.n.ashen

LGBT Romance

AJ Buchannan
Orchestrated Love

Eskay Kabba
Hidden Love
Not So Hidden
Signs of Affection
Deeply Devoted to Him
Honest Love
A Plane and Simple Connection

Lucas LaMont
Roman's Reckoning: Type 6
Mikaél's Moment: Type 6
Stephan's Resurgence: Type 5
Anastasia's Arrival: Type 6

V.C. Willis
The Prince's Priest
The Priest's Assassin
The Assassin's Saint
The Champion's Lord

**Discover more at
4HorsemenPublications.com**

www.ingramcontent.com/pod-product-compliance
Lightning Source LLC
Chambersburg PA
CBHW031550310726
48971CB00008B/2701